Dear Parent:
Your child's love  here!

Every child learns to read ~~~~~~~~~~~~~~~~~~~~~~~~ or her own speed. Some go back and forth between reading levels and read favorite books again and again. Others read through each level in order. You can help your young reader improve and become more confident by encouraging his or her own interests and abilities. From books your child reads with you to the first books he or she reads alone, there are I Can Read Books for every stage of reading:

SHARED READING
Basic language, word repetition, and whimsical illustrations, ideal for sharing with your emergent reader

BEGINNING READING
Short sentences, familiar words, and simple concepts for children eager to read on their own

READING WITH HELP
Engaging stories, longer sentences, and language play for developing readers

READING ALONE
Complex plots, challenging vocabulary, and high-interest topics for the independent reader

ADVANCED READING
Short paragraphs, chapters, and exciting themes for the perfect bridge to chapter books

I Can Read Books have introduced children to the joy of reading since 1957. Featuring award-winning authors and illustrators and a fabulous cast of beloved characters, I Can Read Books set the standard for beginning readers.

A lifetime of discovery begins with the magical words **"I Can Read!"**

Visit www.icanread.com for information
on enriching your child's reading experience.

I Can Read Book® is a trademark of HarperCollins Publishers.

Library of Congress catalog card number: 2011927582
ISBN 978-0-06-207478-2 (trade bdg.)—ISBN 978-0-06-207477-5 (pbk.)

13 14 15 16 LP/WOR 10 9 8 7 6 5 4 3 ❖ First Edition

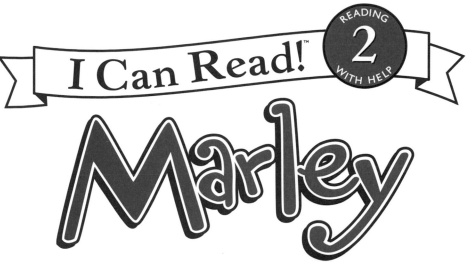

I Can Read!

READING 2 WITH HELP

Marley

NOT A PEEP!

**BASED ON THE BESTSELLING
BOOKS BY JOHN GROGAN**

COVER ART BY RICHARD COWDREY

TEXT BY SUSAN HILL

**INTERIOR ILLUSTRATIONS BY
RICK WHIPPLE**

HARPER
An Imprint of HarperCollinsPublishers

"Marley, we're home," Cassie said.
"We hatched chicks at school
and I got to bring them home
for the weekend."

"Just remember," Mommy said,
"you're in charge of the chicks.
Cute little animals
can be a lot of trouble."
She looked at Marley.
"Isn't that right, Marley?"

"They won't be any trouble at all,"
Cassie promised.

Cassie filled

the special water jar.

She filled the food tray.

"Aren't they cute, Marley?"
she said.

"Woof!"

Marley agreed.

"Cassie, time to go!" Mommy called.

Cassie turned to Marley.

"I have a playdate," she said.

"You're in charge while I'm gone."

Marley looked at the chicks.

He looked at Cassie.

"Woof!"

But nobody looked

at the latch on the cage.

Nobody saw that it was broken.

Marley heard the car drive away.
He heard the chicks moving
quietly in the cage.

He wished he could play
with the chicks.
But they were inside the cage.
He was outside the cage.

Marley went to the living room
to take a nap.
Something woke him.

"Peep."

Marley jumped.

He spun in the air and landed.

"Peep."

It was a baby chick.

"How did you get out of the cage?"

thought Marley.

"Peep."

The chick ran away.

Marley knew he should put the chick

back in the cage.

"I'm in charge," thought Marley.

But he wanted to play.

"It's only one little chick," he thought.

"Peep. Peep, peep."

Marley spun around.

Two more chicks!

"Peep."

Three more chicks!

Suddenly, chicks were everywhere.

Chicks peeping, chicks cheeping.

Chicks hopping, chicks sleeping.

Marley was having so much fun,
he forgot all about being in charge.
Cassie was having a playdate,
and so was Marley.

Just then, Marley heard the car.

Oh, no!

Cassie had said he was in charge.

He had to round up the chicks!

He put one little chick
back in the cage.

Marley ran to round up the others.

"Peep."

Marley turned around.

That chick was right behind him.

How did the chick get free?

The little chicks were so cute,
but they were so much trouble!
How could he get them back
inside the cage to stay?

"Marley!" Mommy cried.

"Woof! Woof!"

Marley tried to explain.

"No, Marley! Not a peep!"

Cassie started to gather the chicks.

"Look, Mommy!" Cassie said.
"Marley tried to be in charge,
but the latch on the cage
is broken."

Mommy and Cassie
put the chicks in the cage
and fixed the latch.
"So cute, and so much trouble,"
said Mommy.

Cassie grinned.

"Just like Marley!"